Copyright © 2010 Flowerpot Press
a Division of Kamalu LLC, Franklin, TN, U.S.A.
and Mitso Media, Inc., Oakville, ON, Canada

American Edition Editor
Sean Kennelly

First Published: 2009

Printed in China.

INTRODUCTION

My First Dictionary is an interesting wordfinder for young children.

It's Easy

My First Dictionary offers a fascinating introduction into the world of words. The design and text are simple and easy-to-follow and provide simple definitions – increasing awareness of words and improving spelling and simple grammar.

Entries and illustrations

My First Dictionary has over 350 entries of carefully chosen words that children commonly come across, or are likely to in the near future. Some of these entries are complemented by matching and informative images.

Objective

The objective of My First Dictionary is to create in children the natural curiousity for words, and also to help them eventually achieve a strong hold over the English language.

A

above
up or higher

act
to do something
or perform a role

academy
institution for the
advancement of
knowledge

addition
adding of numbers
to get a sum

address
an address is where
someone lives or works

adjective
word that describes a
place, thing or person

adult
grown up man
or woman

adverb
an adverb states
'how', 'when',
'where', or 'how
much'. Examples
include *quickly, easily,
mainly,* etc.

afraid
being frightened or
scared

airplane
flying vehicle with
fixed wings and an
engine

alike
when two or more
objects are similar,
they're alike

alligator
large reptile that
has huge jaws
and large teeth

ambulance
vehicle that takes
sick or injured
people to the
hospital

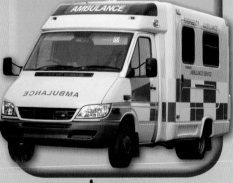

anatomy
science of the body

ant
small, social insects

ape
large tailless primate

arm
part of the human body
between the shoulder
and the elbow

arrows
long, thin objects
with a sharp point

art
art can be anything,
including a painting,
sculpture, drawing,
music, photograph,
or any other form
of expression

astronaut
person whose job
is to explore space

awake
not being asleep

award
something you
get for doing well

awash
covered with water

axe
sharp metal
tool used to
chop wood

n o p q r s t u v w x y z

B

baboon
large monkey with large cheek pouches and a big nose

baby
very young child

bagel
bread roll shaped like a doughnut

banana
sweet, yellow fruit

barn
farm building where animals and their food are kept

batter
uncooked, liquid mixture of eggs, flour, butter and other ingredients. Cakes, cookies and muffins are made from batter

beads
small objects with a hole through them. Used to make jewelry

bear
big, furry animal

blast
sudden and very loud noise

book
composition of words that has been published

brain
organ that helps us to think. The brain is protected by the skull

brave
someone who is not afraid to face dangerous situations

broken
something that has been separated into two or more pieces

broom
object used to sweep the floor

brush
object used to clean, paint or groom

bug
a small insect; a harmful bacteria or virus

bulb
turns electricity into light

burrow
tunnel or hole dug by a small animal

bus
large road vehicle that transports people

C

cab
another name for a taxi

cabbage
leafy plant eaten as a vegetable

cabin
simple house usually made of wood

cake
sweet dessert

camel
large mammal that lives in desert areas

can
container that stores food and drink

candle
stick made of wax that has a wick

cap
type of hat

cast
throw forcefully

chair
piece of furniture that people can sit on

chart
diagram that shows the relationship between things

chimney
structure that funnels smoke away from a fire

chisel
tool with flat blade and sharp edge

circle
round figure where all points are an equal distance from the center

cliff
steep structure of soil and rock

cone
shape that has a point at one end and a circular opening at the other

couple
two similar objects in a pair or two people

courage
quality to face danger or pain without showing too much fear

crane
long-necked bird that lives in wet areas

crawl
moving with body near the ground

cry
to shed tears from the eyes

cub
the young of certain animals, such as lions and bears

cube
geometric figure with six square sides

curtains
material hung to provide a covering or screen

D

dad
another word
for father

dark
opposite of light

daughter
female child

December
last month of the year

deer
long-legged
mammals
that have
hooved feet

desert
very dry area

diamond
very hard,
shiny jewel

dirty
opposite of clean

doctor
person who says
what's wrong with
you when you're ill

dog
pet animals commonly
kept by humans

doll
a small figure kept
as a toy

dollar
currency used in
many countries

dolphin
marine mammal
with teeth and a
long nose

door
entrance to a house
or room

down
opposite of up

drain
a channel or pipe that
carries liquid away

dress
piece of clothing
with a top and a skirt

drill
to make a hole

drop
to let
something fall

drum
musical
instrument

duck
bird that swims
well and lives
near the water

dusk
time of day
after sunset

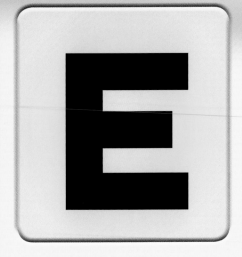

E

earn
to receive something
for working

egg
an oval or round
object laid by most
non-mammal female
creatures

elbow
joint in the middle
of the arm

eleven
ten plus one

emperor
ruler of a country

empty
containing nothing

entrance
an opening

eager
having or showing
keen interest or desire

eagle
large bird of prey
with a hooked beak
and sharp talons

elephant
largest land animal, with
a long trunk

engine
a machine with moving parts that moves an object

envelope
folded paper or card to contain letters and other items

eraser
object used to rub off pencil marks

Europe
continent in the Northern Hemisphere, including the England, Ireland, Italy, Germany, France and Spain

excellent
very good; outstanding

exercise
physical or mental exertion that is done to improve health and performance

extinct
to have died-out as a species. Extinct animals include dodos and dinosaurs

F

face
front of the head with features such as the mouth and nose

factory
a building where things are made or put together

falcon
bird of prey that hunts other birds and small animals

family
group of people who are related to each other

famous
very well known

farmer
person who looks after animals and produces food by growing plants

fast
ability to act or move quickly

fawn
young deer

fear
to be afraid or scared

femur
upper leg bone, which is the longest in the human body

fin
fish have fins that help them swim

firefighter
person who puts out fires and saves lives

flag

square or rectangular piece of material that represents a country, state, province, or city

flower

the part of the plant containing the organs that make new plants, usually surrounded by petals

foal

young horse

fork

object with prongs used for eating solid food

fraction

part of a whole. Half of an orange is a fraction of an orange

fruit

part of some plants that contain seeds. Apples and oranges are fruits

funnel

conical shaped structure with a wide opening at one end and a narrow opening at the other

furniture

tables, beds and chairs are all furniture

furrow

a long narrow trench in the ground for planting seeds or helping water drain

future

time that is yet to come

G

geyser
natural hot spring that sprays steam and water above the ground

gibbon
small, tree-dwelling ape found in Asia

garden
man-made area where plants and flowers grow

gazelle
a small slender antelope found in Africa and Asia

gate
a hinged barrier in a fence

geography
study of the location of people and features on earth

giddy
having a dizzying sensation

gather
to collect

gnat
small flying insect

gold
precious metal. Some coins and jewellery are made of gold

golf
sport where a ball is hit into a series of holes using metal sticks called clubs

grandparents
the mother and father of each of your parents

grass
common plant that forms a green covering over the ground

grate
to make into very small shreds

guest
visitor to a house

guitar
musical instrument, usually with six or 12 strings and a fingerboard with frets to create different chords

gift
something you give someone without asking anything in return

give
when you let someone have something, you 'give' the person that thing

glasses
objects used to help people see more clearly

glue
substance that sticks things together

H

habitat
natural place where animals and plants live

hail
pellets of frozen rain that fall from clouds

ham
meat from a pig's leg that is salted and dried or smoked

hamster
small rodent sometimes kept as a pet

harp
musical instrument with many strings

hat
a shaped covering, worn on the head

hatchet
axe with a short handle

haystack
big pile of hay

heart
an organ made of muscle that pumps blood around the body

hem
a sewn edge of a piece of material

herbivore
plant-eating animal

hero
person with courage and character who is known for their good deeds

hoe
garden tool with
a long handle and
flat blade

hoof
hard, protective
covering on the
feet of some animals.
Deer, zebras and
horses have hooves

honey
a sweet, sticky
liquid made by
bees from nectar

hornet
wasp-like flying
insect capable of
stinging

hose
flexible pipe
through which water
flows, usually used to
water plants

hound
a dog bred to track
animals by scent

hurricane
dangerous storm
with fast winds
and heavy rainfall

hyena
meat-eating animal
that hunts and
scavenges prey

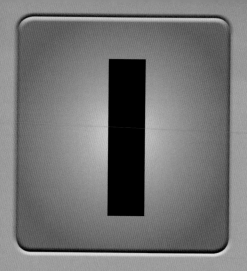

I

iceberg
a large floating mass of ice that has separated from an ice sheet

icicle
hanging ice that forms when dripping water freezes over time

igloo
house made from blocks of ice

impala
a graceful antelope found in large herds in southern Africa

infant
a very young child or baby

irate
feeling or showing great anger

island
piece of land surrounded by water

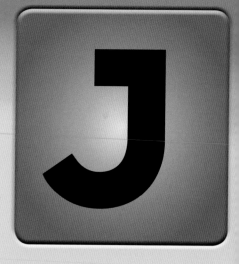

J

jacket
short coat

janitor
someone who cleans a building

K

kidney
bean-shaped organs in the human body that helps to produce urine

kilt
traditional dress worn by the people of Scotland

kiwi fruit
fuzzy brown egg-shaped fruit with a slightly sour green center

jab
poke abruptly

jet
fast and powerful airplane

jewel
precious stone

judo
a form of martial arts

junk
traditional Chinese sailing ship build from wood

justice
when something is treated fairly and reasonably

kangaroo
a large marsupial with powerful back legs found in Australia

kayak
small, narrow boat

kennel
shelter for dogs

knee
part of the body where the leg bends

M

macaroni
narrow tubes of pasta

magician
An artist who performs magic is known as a magician. Magic is the art of performing illusions and tricks

magnifying glass
lens that can make things look bigger than their actual size

mailbox
box where letters are put

mammal
typically any warm-blooded animal with hair or fur. Mammals nourish their young with milk

mammoth
large, elephant-like animal of the Ice Ages

marsh
wet and grassy land

marsupial
mammals with pouches, where the young are kept. Kangaroos and koalas are marsupials

meal
good amount of food eaten at one time

medal
award given for a good performance

metal
shiny, solid element that can conduct heat and electricity. Gold, copper, silver and iron are metals

mountain
natural elevation from the earth's surface that is higher than a hill

mittens
thick gloves that keep the hands warm

mole
burrowing mammal with powerful claws and poor eyesight

mosaic
work of art made up of pieces of glass, tiles, stones, or other objects fitted together

moth
nocturnal flying insect related to butterflies

muffin
small cake

mummy
preserved dead body usually related to Ancient Egypt

museum
a building where objects of interest are displayed

N

nail
hard surface that grows at the end of the fingers and toes

nag
bother or worry persistently

nanny
person employed to care for a child in their own home

nap
short sleep during the day

napkin
something with which you clean your face after eating

narrow
not very wide, usually in relation to an object's length or height

neat
clean and proper

neighbor
someone living close to your house

neon
gas that is used in some lights

nest ....
structure made of twigs where birds lay eggs and take care of their young

new
condition of something that has never been used before

newspaper
printed publication that gives information about current events of public interest

newt
bright-colored amphibian

nib
the pointed end part of a pen

nightingale
bird that is known for singing beautiful songs

nocturnal
condition of being more active at night than the daytime. Bats are nocturnal creatures

nod
the up and down movement of the head

noodles
strips of pasta or similar dough, typically made with eggs

note
short written message

noun
word that represents a person, place or thing

nurse
person that looks after you when you are sick

nut
fruit with a hard shell

nutmeg
seed of a tropical tree that is used as a spice

O

oil
a thick, sticky liquid made from petroleum

oar
tool generally made of wood that is used to row a boat

observatory
place from where people observe the skies, using tools such as telescopes

ocean
a very large expanse of sea

octopus
creature that has eight arms covered in suction cups

olive
small oval fruit

Olympics
the Olympic games began in ancient Greece over 2,700 years ago. The games are held every four years

omnivore
animal that eats both plants and meat. Humans are omnivores

omit
to leave out

orbit
fixed path that one object takes to circle around another. The moon orbits the earth, and the earth orbits the sun

orca
a large toothed member of the dolphin family with black and white markings, also known as a killer whale

orchid
colorful flower that grows in warm areas

ostrich
largest bird in the world

otter
playful aquatic mammal

ounce
unit of weight that is one-twelfth of a pound

oval
rounded egg shape

oven
an enclosed compartment used for cooking food

ox
another name for a cow or bull

overcoat
long warm coat worn over clothing

oyster
soft-bodied mollusk with a hard protective shell often eaten raw as a delicacy

ozone
colorless toxic gas that forms a protective layer from the sun in our atmosphere

P

pebble
small, smooth stone

package
object or objects, placed in a box or wrapped for transport

paddle
a short oar used for rowing a small boat

pail
container with a handle

palette
thin board, on which an artist mixes paint

party
social gathering of invited guests

pentagon
five-sided shape

pepper
spice people use on their food

pod
group of whales

proverb
short saying that is a commonly known truth

pupil
person who is learning in a school

puppet
small doll that is made to move by pulling strings

puzzle
game that requires logic and knowledge to solve it

qualm
feeling of doubt and uneasiness

quack
the sound of a duck

quarter
the portion of something when divided equally into four; coin worth 25 cents

quicksand
loose, wet sand where objects can sink

quiet
calm or without noise

quilt
a warm bed covering made of padding between layers of fabric stitched together

quip
to make a joke or a witty remark

quit
give up; go away or leave

quiver
container where arrows are kept

quiz
a test of knowledge

R

rake
garden tool that helps to collect leaves and grass

rabbit
small mammal with big ears

racket
loud and disturbing noise

radar
device that is used to locate objects at a distance

radio
communication device where you can listen to music and talk shows

radius
distance from the center of a circle to the border

raisin
dried grape

rattle
series of short, rapid knocking sounds

recipe
set of instructions for making a particular dish, usually of food

a b c d e f g h i j k l m

reef
a ridge of jagged rock, coral or sand just above or below the surface of the sea

refrigerator
machine that keeps food cold and fresh

rein
strap that a rider controls and steers a horse with

rhinoceros
large, thick-skinned animal with one or two horns on its head

rhyme
to have similar sounds, like 'kite' and 'light', 'bite' and 'right' etc.

robot
machine programmed to move automatically and perform specific functions

rocket
a tube filled with fuel that can be propelled to great heights

rodent
mammal whose two front teeth grow constantly. Mice, squirrels, hamsters, and rats are all rodents

roof
covering of a room or building

roost
to sit on a perch

rooster
male chicken

roots
plant parts below the ground that get water and other nutrients from the soil

route
the way or course taken to get to a destination

rug
floor covering made of thick fabric

S

scroll
a roll of parchment or paper for writing or painting on

shrub
low-lying bush with a woody stem

silk
delicate thread used to make fine fabric

sill
wood that forms the base of a window

sack
container made of fabric, paper or plastic that you can put things in

sail
large piece of strong fabric that catches wind and helps a boat move through the water

scallop
an edible mollusk with a ribbed, fan-shaped shell

seal
a device or substance that joins two items together

season
a time of year like winter, spring, summer, and autumn with particular weather patterns and daylight hours

silo
a tower or pit used to store grain

skull
bony structure of the head that protects the brain

sleet
freezing rain

slither
to move smoothly and without obstruction

shovel
tool used to dig and move material

snail
a mollusk with a spiral shell that the whole body can be withdrawn into

steak
slice of meat or fish for grilling or frying

swap
to give something in exchange for something else

strait
narrow body of water connecting two bigger bodies of water

synthesizer
musical instrument that electronically creates sounds

snap
to break something in two, usually with a cracking sound

swamp
wet area that usually has a lot of animal and plant life

soil
the upper layer of earth in which plants grow

sphere
ball-shaped object

T

tablet
a flat slab of stone, clay or wood

tambourine
shallow drum with metal discs used as a percussion instrument

toddler
a young child just beginning to walk

telescope
instrument through which distant objects appear closer

tent
shelter made of fabric that can be moved

thunder
a loud rumbling or crashing sound heard after lightning due to rapidly expanding air

tie
narrow band of fabric that is tied around the neck

tongs
simple pincer tool used to pick things up

tornado
rapidly spinning air that is shaped like a funnel

town
urban area smaller than a city

tract
large area of land

a b c d e f g h i j k l m

tractor
powerful farm vehicle, usually with large treaded wheels

trail
rough path

triangle
a shape with three straight sides

trout
a fish of the salmon family often fished for food

truce
state of peace between two opposing parties

trunk
tree's major support

trust
to be confident about and have faith in something

tub
large vessel for holding or storing liquids

tuck
to push, fold or turn something to hold it in place

tugboat
sturdy boat that guides other bigger boats in and out of harbors

twister
another name for a tornado – rapidly spinning air that can be very dangerous

X

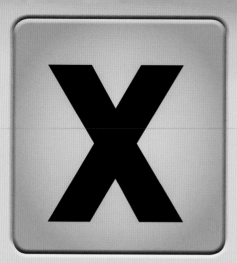

x-ray
special picture of your teeth or bones taken in a hospital, doctor or a dentists' office

xylophone
musical instrument with rows of bars often made of wood

Y

yacht
a medium-sized boat with sails

yak
large wild ox with shaggy hair, humped shoulders and large horns

yam
another name for the sweet potato, a vegetable

yard
small area of land attached to a house

yardstick
a measuring stick equal to one yard, or three feet, in length

yarn
cord of twisted fiber that is used in weaving and sewing

yell
to shout in a loud voice

yelp
bark in a high-pitched tone

yolk
yellow portion of an egg

yo-yo
a round toy attached to a string

Z

zebra
horse-like animal
with black and
white stripes

zeal
great energy or
enthusiasm in pursuit
of a cause or objective

zero
no quantity or
number; none

zigzag
line or course
with abrupt left
and right turns

zipper
two strips of metal or
plastic that are joined
together with a slider

zoologist
scientist who
studies animals

ACTIVITIES

Match the following words to the pictures

xylophone

noodles

shovel

whisk

olives

trout

Fill In The Blanks

(Tip: Look back through the dictionary to help you if you're not sure of an answer)

The object you use to sweep the floor is called a _____.

A _____ is a large mammal that lives in desert areas.

_____ is hot liquid rock that comes out of volcanoes.

The _____ is a burrowing mammal that does not see very well.

A small, smooth stone is called a _____.

Freezing rain is also known as _____.

The tool that is used to turn nuts and bolts is called a _____.